Little Sister

Karen's Witch

Ann M. Martin

Illustrations by Susan Tang

A
LITTLE APPLE
PAPERBACK

SCHOLASTIC INC.
New York Toronto London Auckland Sydney

No part of this publication may be reproduced in whole or in part, or stored in a retrieval system, or transmitted in any form or by any means, electronic, mechanical, photocopying, recording, or otherwise, without written permission of the publisher. For information regarding permission, write to Scholastic Inc., 555 Broadway, New York, NY 10012.

ISBN 0-590-48463-X

Copyright © 1988 by Ann M. Martin. All rights reserved. Published by Scholastic Inc. APPLE PAPERBACKS is a registered trademark of Scholastic Inc. BABY-SITTERS LITTLE SISTER is a trademark of Scholastic Inc.

12 11 10 9 8 7 6 5 4 3 2 1   8   4 5 6 7 8 9/9

Printed in the U.S.A.   40

For
Laura Elizabeth,
the newest Perkins

Karen's Witch

Karen's Two Families

Hi.

I am Karen Brewer.

I'm six going on seven years old, and I think I'm very lucky.

I'm lucky because I have two families. Most people only have one. But my brother Andrew and I have two.

I have two of lots of other things. I have two houses. One is little and one is big. (There is one for each family.) I have two pairs of pink sneakers. (One for each house.) And I have two teddy bears and two baby

dolls and two pairs of jeans. I even have two pieces of Tickly, my special blanket. I ripped Tickly in half so I could have a piece at each house.

"Aren't we lucky?" I asked Andrew one day. Andrew is only four. I'm his big sister. This is a very important job.

"Yup," said Andrew. But I think he didn't mean it. He doesn't always like having two families. Sometimes I don't, either. It can get confusing.

2

At the little house live Mommy and Seth. Seth is our stepfather.

He likes animals.

When Seth married our mother and moved to the little house, he brought his dog and cat along. His cat is named Rocky. His dog is named Midgie. These are stupid names. I would have named the cat Jones and the dog Vance. Jones and Vance are really great names.

At the big house live a whole bunch of people. The most important person there is our daddy. Then there's Elizabeth. She's married to Daddy, so she's our stepmother.

Mommy and Daddy got divorced. Then they each got married again. That's how come Andrew and I have a mother, a stepmother, a father, and a stepfather.

At the big house, also, are Elizabeth's four kids. They are my stepbrothers and stepsister.

Sam and Charlie are old. They go to high school.

David Michael is seven. He is just about

my age. Sometimes he thinks he's so great because he gets to live with my daddy all the time.

And then there's Kristy. She's thirteen. She is one of my most favorite people.

Finally, there are Shannon and Boo-Boo, my other dog and cat. Shannon is a frisky puppy. (She sort of belongs to David Michael, but I try to forget that.) Boo-Boo is an old fat cat. He's mean. (I don't like him much.)

Here are the good things about having two families: Two birthday parties, two Christmases, and all those other two's.

Someone can always take care of you when you are sick.

Mommy won't let Andrew and me eat candy, but Daddy will. So we fill up at his house.

Here are the bad things about having two families: Different rules. At Mommy's house, *always* put your toys back in the toy box. No running indoors. No Saturday morning cartoons.

At Daddy's house, never leave the TV on if you're not watching it. Keep the closet doors shut. No spying on the neighbors. (I forget the spying rule a lot.)

Plus, no matter how hard I try, I always end up with two somethings at one house — and no something at the other. One time I was *sure* I had lost the party shoes that stay at Daddy's house. So I brought over the ones from Mommy's house. Then I found the first pair under my bed. And I forgot to take the second pair back to Mommy's. When it was time for a party at Mommy's house, I had to wear my pink sneakers. Mommy was mad.

So was I.

Andrew and I only live at the big house every other weekend. The rest of the time we live at the little house. The little house is a good place to be if you like peace and quiet. The big house is usually noisy. It's usually busy. Someone there will always play with me.

Also, a witch lives next door.

I am not kidding. I know because I spy on her all the time. Daddy's rule is *no spying,* but I can't help it. I *have* to spy on her. If you lived next door to a witch, wouldn't you spy? It's important to know what she's up to. I have to protect my family. A witch is scary, but interesting.

The witch says her name is Mrs. Porter, but her real name (her witch name) is Morbidda Destiny. Doesn't that sound spooky? Morbidda Destiny wears long black robes. She smells funny. Her hair is wild and wispy and gray. She planted an herb garden in her yard. She uses those herbs to put spells on people. And animals.

"She put three spells on Boo-Boo this year," I told Kristy.

Kristy rolled her eyes. She doesn't believe Morbidda Destiny is a witch.

Here is a fact: Even when you're thirteen, you don't know everything. *I* know about Morbidda Destiny. I know she's a witch. And I know enough to be careful.

Going to Daddy's

One Friday afternoon, Mommy drove Andrew and me over to Daddy's. It was time for our weekend with him.

"'Bye, Mommy!" I called as Andrew and I hopped out of the car. "See you on Sunday!"

It was almost suppertime. The sky was dark. As we ran to the front door, I said to Andrew, "Doesn't it feel like fall to you?"

"Yup," he replied. "But it isn't."

"I know, but doesn't it *feel* like it?"

"Yup."

"It's all gray and chilly. The wind is blowing. And look at that huge full moon. It's Halloween."

"Not really."

"But it *feels* like it." I glanced at Morbidda Destiny's house next door. It was gloomy and dark. Only one light was on. I thought I could see the witch moving around inside, but I wasn't sure.

"It's a good night for witching," I added.

Andrew didn't answer. Sometimes I make up stories that scare him. I hoped I wasn't scaring him now. I never mean to.

I threw open the door of Daddy's house. "Hello, everybody!" I shouted. "We're here!"

Kristy was the first one to run into the hallway. "Hi, you guys," she replied. She hugged me tightly. Then she hugged Andrew.

"Ooh, Kristy, it's a Halloween night tonight," I said in a low, spooky voice. "I bet Morbidda Destiny — Oh, hi, Daddy!" I stopped talking about the witch. Daddy and

Elizabeth had come into the hall. I didn't want them to think I'd been spying.

My stepbrothers came, too. There were lots of hugs and hellos.

"Come put your knapsacks away," Daddy said to Andrew and me.

So we did. I forgot about Morbidda Destiny for awhile. I was very busy getting settled. There was so much to do. I had to check on my dolls and Tickly. I had to say hi to Shannon and Boo-Boo. And I had to see if anything interesting was going on in David Michael's room. (Sometimes he keeps bugs in jars.)

Then it was dinnertime. We ate in the kitchen. And then people began to leave. Sam and Charlie went to a dance at their high school. Daddy and Elizabeth went to the movies.

Kristy baby-sat for us that night. She was in charge of Andrew and David Michael and me. Baby-sitting is one of the things Kristy does best. She always thinks of fun stuff to do.

We were in the middle of a game of Old Maid when I heard mewing at the front door. "That's Boo-Boo," I said. "I better let him in."

I ran to the door. I opened it wide.

Right away, I wished I hadn't opened it at all.

The Witch Next Door

Standing on the front steps was Morbidda Destiny's black cat, Midnight.

"Aughhh!" I screamed.

"Purr-row?" asked Midnight. He blinked his round yellow eyes.

"What is it?" Kristy called.

I could hear her running to the door. But I was too scared to say a word, so I didn't answer her.

What was Midnight doing on our front steps? I wondered. It must mean something. Midnight was a sign of bad things to come.

Or maybe the cat wasn't Midnight at all.
Maybe it was Morbidda Destiny in the form
of a cat!

"Aughhh!" I shrieked again, just as Kristy
ran to my side.

Kristy looked out the door. She looked
right at Midnight. Then she looked beyond
Midnight, into the gardens and across the
lawn.

"What's the matter?" she asked.

"What's the *matter?*" I cried. Couldn't

Kristy see for herself? *"That* is the matter."
I pointed to the cat. Midnight blinked at me
again.

"Midnight?" said Kristy. "So what? He's
just sitting there. He probably wants to play
with Boo-Boo."

"But Kristy, that's the witch's cat! Or
maybe it's the witch herself. And he's blink-
ing at me. I know he's here to put me under
a spell. Maybe Morbidda Destiny wants to
turn *me* into a cat."

"Now why would she want to do that?"
asked Kristy. She closed the door. Then she
smiled at me.

I couldn't smile back. This was serious.

"Let's finish our game," said Kristy. "Andrew and David Michael are waiting for
us."

I sighed. Then I shivered. I could feel
goose bumps on my arms. "Kristy, I'm
scared," I said.

"Oh, Karen. Everything is all right. Really."
Kristy held my hand as we walked back to
the living room.

The living room was where we were playing cards. Andrew and I have a big playroom on the second floor of the house, but sometimes we like to play in the living room. Daddy always lets us. That's the kind of person he is. He doesn't worry about silly things.

Andrew and David Michael were sitting on the floor, holding their cards.

"What took you so long?" David Michael asked when Kristy and I got back.

David Michael sounded cross. That happens sometimes. He thinks he's so great — just because he's a little older than I am.

"For your information," I began. (*For your information* is something Kristy says a lot, so I knew it was very grown-up.) I liked the way it sounded. I said it again. "For your information, it was not Boo-Boo at the door."

"Who was it then?" asked Andrew.

"It was . . . Midnight," I replied. I used my low, spooky voice.

"Morbidda Destiny's cat?" shrieked David Michael.

I nodded.

"You guys," said Kristy, "what is the big deal?"

"The big deal is that a witch's cat — " began David Michael.

"Or maybe the witch herself," I interrupted.

" — was right on our front porch. Midnight has never come over here before." David Michael crossed his arms.

"I wonder why he chose tonight?" I asked softly. "Maybe because there's a full moon. The wind is blowing. It's a witchy, Halloween night."

Andrew scampered into Kristy's lap. He stuck his thumb in his mouth.

"I think you're scaring your brother," Kristy told me.

Witch Stories

"Kristy," I said, "let's not play Old Maid. Let's read stories."

Andrew took his thumb out of his mouth. "But not witch stories," he said. He put his thumb back in his mouth.

"I *want* witch stories," I said.

"I know a witch story that's not scary," Kristy told us. "It's called *The Tooth Witch*. It's about a good witch who becomes the Tooth Fairy."

David Michael said the story sounded boring. Kristy read it anyway. Andrew and

I liked it a lot. And David Michael changed his mind and said it was funny.

"Now I want another witch story," I said.

"Not me," said Andrew. "No more witch stories."

"Not me," said David Michael. "No more stories at all."

"It's bedtime anyway," said Kristy. "Go on upstairs and brush your teeth. All three of you. And Karen, when you're ready for bed, I'll read you *The Littlest Witch*. Is that a deal?"

"Deal!" I agreed.

Andrew and David Michael and I went upstairs. We went to our bedrooms and changed into our pajamas. Then we met in the bathroom. We always brush our teeth together. This was my idea.

We crowded around the sink. We squeezed as much toothpaste onto our brushes as we could. Then we brushed very hard. We brushed until our mouths were so full of toothpaste that we couldn't hold it in anymore.

"Okay!" I said. "One, two, three, spit!" Only my mouth was so full that it sounded like I said, "Unh, two, fee, pit!"

We leaned over the sink and spit out our toothpaste at the same time.

"Look at all that foam," I said.

"I think we set a record," David Michael added.

We watched the foam until we heard Kristy's footsteps on the stairs. Then I turned on the water. I rinsed the foam away. Nobody, not even Kristy, knows how we brush our teeth.

"Bedtime!" Kristy called.

David Michael and Andrew dashed into their rooms. I dashed into mine, too. I jumped into bed and grabbed Tickly and Moosie, my stuffed cat. I held them tightly while I waited for Kristy.

Kristy said good night to David Michael and to Andrew. Then she came into my room. She headed straight for the bookcase and found *The Littlest Witch*. It was easy to find. It's one of my favorite stories, so it's always at the end of the row of witch books.

Kristy climbed onto my bed. She put her arm around me, and I rested my head on her shoulder. I knew *The Littlest Witch* so well that I could tell myself the whole story without even opening the book. But I liked to hear Kristy read it.

When it was over, I said, "I would like that book even better if we didn't have our own witch right next door."

"We don't," said Kristy.

"We do," I told her.

Kristy kissed me on the nose. "Good night," she said. "Stop thinking about witches."

"Good night," I answered.

But I could not stop thinking about witches. I just couldn't.

Shivers and Goose Bumps

Kristy turned on my night-light. Then she left my room. She closed the door, but not all the way. I like to see a streak of light from the hallway.

I lay back in my bed. I looked at my night-light. It is shaped like Donald Duck. We got it at Disney World. I looked at the light around my doorway. Perfect. Plenty of light.

Do you want to know a secret? I am afraid of the dark. Not *very* afraid, just a little afraid. Well, maybe more than a little afraid. But I don't think I'm a baby about it.

I turned over onto my stomach. I smushed up my pillow. I flattened it out.

I was not sleepy.

I played a game with myself. I tried to remember everything that had happened since I said, "See you on Sunday!" to Mommy.

Well, first I had looked over at Morbidda Destiny's house. I thought I could see her in the window. Then I had told Andrew that tonight felt like Halloween.

I shivered and got goose bumps on my arms again. Witches . . . Halloween . . . black cats . . . spells.

I sat up and looked out my window. Guess what I can see from my bedroom? Morbidda Destiny's house. It was all dark and silent. Oooh, spooky.

Now I had goose bumps on my arms *and* legs.

I turned on my light.

"Karen, what are you doing?" called Kristy. She must have seen the light from out in the hallway.

"Nothing," I answered.

I turned off the light.

I lay on my back, my front, my right side, my left side. I did not feel a speck sleepy.

I thought: Morbidda Destiny is a witch. That is a fact. I've seen her lots and lots of times in her witchy black clothes. I've seen her funny hair. I've seen her herbs. And I've seen her broom. But do you know something strange? I've never seen her *ride* the broom.

Isn't that weird? All witches ride brooms.

I sat up and looked out my window again. Maybe witches only ride brooms at night. That would make sense. If they rode them in the daytime, people would see them. They might get arrested by the police.

I decided to watch Morbidda Destiny's house until I saw her get on her broomstick and start to ride into the night. Then I would call Kristy. When Kristy saw Mrs. Porter riding a broom, she would finally believe that she wasn't *just* Mrs. Porter. She was a true witch.

I rested my arms on my windowsill and watched and watched. I saw the branches of the trees moving. I saw a car drive down the street. But Morbidda Destiny's house was quiet.

I sat up for so long that I began to feel sleepy.

My head started to nod. . . .

The Witch at Night

Suddenly I sat up straight.

Something was going on next door. The highest window of the house was opening slowly. The window was on a side of the house, facing me. I had a good view.

Slowly, slowly, up, up it went.

And then a wooden stick poked through the window. No, it wasn't a stick. It was a broom handle!

It poked farther and farther out. The next thing I saw was Morbidda Destiny. She was

riding on the broom! Midnight was sitting in front of her. He looked right over at me and blinked his yellow eyes.

"Heh, heh, heh," cackled Morbidda Destiny. Then she whizzed off into the dark night.

I screamed. Loudly.

A few moments later I heard footsteps on the stairs.

"Karen, Karen! What's wrong?" cried Kristy.

She dashed into my room and turned the light on.

"Are you sick?" she asked. "Did you hurt yourself?"

I could hardly talk.

"Turn off the light," was the first thing I said.

Kristy turned off the light.

"Now come look out the window," I told her. "Hurry."

Kristy plopped onto my bed. She leaned over and peered out the window. I sat next to her and peered out, too.

"I don't see anything," said Kristy.

"Me neither." I felt terrible.

"Then why did you scream?"

"Because . . . because Mrs. Porter really *is* Morbidda Destiny, the witch. I saw her and Midnight fly out that window on a broomstick." I pointed to the window. It wasn't even open anymore. Now I felt worse.

"Oh, Karen," said Kristy. "You must have been dreaming."

27

"I *wasn't!* I hadn't gone to sleep yet."

"Are you *sure?* You went to bed an awfully long time ago."

"I did?" I said. I remembered that I had felt sleepy. But I had not gone to sleep. I knew I hadn't. I didn't think Kristy would believe me, though.

"Karen, how would you like to sleep in my room tonight?" Kristy asked. "Would you feel better if you were with me?"

"Can I bring Donald Duck and Moosie and Tickly?" I asked.

"Sure," said Kristy. "We'll leave the door open. And I'm going to pull the shades down so we can't see outside."

"I'd like that," I said. The goose bumps were gone.

I followed Kristy down the hall to her bedroom. Pad, pad, pad, pad. I like to walk in bare feet.

Kristy put her nightgown on, and I plugged Donald Duck in. Then we both climbed into her big bed. I hugged Moosie and Tickly.

"Are you sleepy yet?" asked Kristy.

"No. I'm too scared."

"Still?"

"A little."

Moosie and I snuggled closer to Kristy. "I'm glad we can't see outside," I said. I shivered.

"Karen, I've never seen you so scared. Calm down."

"I can't. Mrs. Porter is a witch," I said. I felt like crying. "Open your door wider. Please?"

Kristy got up and opened her door wider.

I didn't feel safe until she was back in bed.

"I'll tell you a story," said Kristy. "Once upon a time . . ."

I must have been sleepy after all. I don't remember anything that happened in that story after "Once upon a time."

Spying

When I woke up the next morning, I was surprised to find myself in Kristy's big bed. Kristy was next to me. She was asleep on her back. Moosie was on her chest. I wondered how he got there. As Kristy breathed in and out, Moosie rode up and down.

Then I looked around the room. Kristy's door was open. Her shades were pulled down. Donald Duck was plugged in by the bed.

Suddenly I remembered what had happened the night before. I remembered not being able to fall asleep. And I remembered Morbidda Destiny riding away on her broomstick.

I leaped out of bed. I ran down the hallway to my room and looked out the window. The sun was shining. Thank goodness. In all that brightness, it was hard to be scared.

I checked Morbidda Destiny's house. It was quiet. The upstairs window was still closed. There was no sign of Midnight or a broom or anything witchy.

I changed into my jeans and a sweatshirt and went downstairs.

"Good morning!" I called to anyone who might be up.

"Good morning," answered Elizabeth. Her voice came from the kitchen.

David Michael and Andrew were eating breakfast with Elizabeth. Boo-Boo and Shannon were having their breakfast, too.

"Where's Daddy?" I asked.

"He's working in the garden," Elizabeth told me. She kissed me good morning as I

31

sat down at the table. "He's out front. What would you like for breakfast?"

"Do we have any Crunch-O cereal?" I asked.

"I think so," said Elizabeth.

Goody, I thought. I could tell this was going to be a special day. Something interesting was going to happen.

As soon as I'd eaten breakfast, I went outside to check on Morbidda Destiny's house. I wasn't spying — exactly. Just looking around a little. But Daddy might have thought I was spying, so I made sure to stay in back, since he was in front.

First I stood behind a rosebush and looked at the side of Morbidda Destiny's house.

Nothing.

Then I moved to the very edge of our yard and stood behind our toolshed. I looked at the back of Morbidda Destiny's house.

Nothing.

I ran all the way inside, up to my room, and looked out my window again.

Still nothing. Not a sign of life next door.

"Karen?" said Kristy's voice.

I whirled around.

"What are you doing?" she asked.

"Looking at Morbidda Destiny's house. You know what? I don't think she's at home," I told Kristy.

"So?"

"I don't think she ever came back after she flew off last night. And you know what that means, don't you?"

"What?" asked Kristy with a sigh.

Kristy sounded the way most big people sound when I talk about my witch who lives next door.

"It means she's at a witch meeting," I told her. "Something is going to happen. Soon."

Kristy shook her head. "Karen, Karen, Karen," she said.

"Kristy, Kristy, Kristy," I replied.

We both laughed. But I was feeling nervous — and a little scared.

Playing Witch

Luckily, the doorbell rang then. I ran to answer it. But before I opened the door, I paused. What if it was Morbidda Destiny, back from her meeting?

"Who is it?" I called.

"It's Hannie!"

"Oh, Hannie! Goody!" I threw open the door. Hannie Papadakis is my best friend when I'm at Daddy's house. We're in the same class at school. (At Mommy's house, my best friend is Nancy Dawes. She's my best best friend. She's in our class, too, and she lives next door to Mommy and Seth, so I see her lots more than I see Hannie.)

But I was glad Hannie had come over. Of course, I told her all about Morbidda Destiny and her broomstick and the witch meeting.

"Oooh," said Hannie softly. She looked scared.

"Hey!" I exclaimed. "Let's pretend we're witches. Wouldn't that be fun?"

"Okay," said Hannie. Hannie almost always does what I say.

We went to the playroom and opened the dress-up box. We put on tall black hats. Then we each found a broom. I made sure Daddy was still in the front yard. Then Hannie and I went into the backyard.

"We need Boo-Boo," I said. "We have to make him sit on one of the brooms."

"There he is!" said Hannie.

Boo-Boo was napping under a bush.

"Wake up, wake up," I ordered Boo-Boo. I placed my broom in front of him. "Get on the broomstick."

Boo-Boo opened one eye. Then he closed it again. He was very sleepy.

"Oh, never mind," I said. "Come on, Hannie. You be Witchy Witch and I'll be Samantha Twitchit. Now let's make up witch rhymes."

"Witch rhymes?"

"Yes. Listen to this one," I said.

> "Witch, witch.
> You give me a twitch."

"You make my ear itch," added Hannie. We laughed. Then I said,

"Witching time, witching time.
Making up a witching rhyme."

We edged closer to Morbidda Destiny's herb garden. Hannie peeked into it cautiously.

I was still working on rhymes.

"The witch at night,
she gave me a fright.
She was a very scary si — "

"Shhh!" hissed Hannie. "Listen."

I listened. I heard rustling in the herb garden. Then I saw something black and heard a cackle. "Heh, heh, heh."

I grabbed Hannie's hand.. We weren't alone. Someone else was in the garden.

And I thought I knew who it was.

The Witch and Her Cat

"It's Morbidda Destiny!" I whispered loudly to Hannie.

"Oh, noooo . . ."

The witch was bending over. She was carrying a basket in one hand, and she was filling it with herbs from her garden. She kept snipping away at things with a little pair of scissors.

Snip, snip. Snip, snip.

My heart began to beat faster. I was practically right next to the witch. Luckily, she didn't know it.

Morbidda Destiny's frazzly hair was blowing in the wind. So were her long black robes and her black shawl.

"Where are her hat and her broomstick?" whispered Hannie.

I shrugged. "I guess she doesn't need them in the garden."

"Heh, heh, heh," cackled my witch.

"Oooh. Let's get out of here!" said Hannie softly. She reached for my hand. I gave it a squeeze. I knew just how she felt. My heart was pounding so loudly I was sure Morbidda Destiny could hear it.

"Come *on*," said Hannie. "She knows we're here. She's cackling at us."

Just then I heard a soft meow.

"No, she isn't," I said. "At least, I don't think she is. She's cackling at Midnight. I can see him now."

I knew that what I was doing was spying. I couldn't help it. I just *had* to hear what Morbidda Destiny was saying. Maybe she would say something about her witch meeting.

But first the witch had to do some more cackling.

"Heh, heh, heh. Heh, heh, heh."

Snip, snip. Snip, snip.

Suddenly Morbidda Destiny took a step forward. Hannie and I jumped back. We were still hidden. *Whew.*

"Midnight," Morbidda Destiny muttered.

Midnight looked at her with his round yellow eyes.

"Twelve o'clock," she said.

Snip, snip. She took another step forward.

Hannie and I backed up. We were holding hands tightly.

"Midnight," Morbidda Destiny muttered again.

Did she mean her cat or the middle of the night? I wondered.

"Important meeting," I heard my witch murmur. She peered over at her cat. The cat opened its mouth and meowed loudly.

My stomach began to feel funny.

"Company coming," said Morbidda Destiny.

My stomach felt worse.

"Mrow," said Midnight.

"Ouch!" said Hannie.

"What? What?" I whispered.

"You're holding my hand too tight. You're going to squeeze my fingers off."

"Sorry."

Morbidda Destiny was talking again. "Yes, yes. We must be ready," she said.

And all at once I knew what she was talking about.

The Witching Hour

"Oh! Oh, no! Oh, my gosh!" I cried. I was so scared I forgot to be quiet.

"What's that? Who's there?" called Morbidda Destiny.

Hannie gasped loudly.

It was time to leave.

I pulled Hannie away from the garden. We ran all the way to my house. We didn't stop until we were inside. But on the way, we tossed off our hats. We left them beside the brooms. I would have to remember to bring the hats and brooms inside later.

"Hannie, this is terrible!" I exclaimed, as we ran through the back door.

"I know. She almost caught us."

"Not that. That's not the terrible part."

Hannie and I sat down in the kitchen. Shannon was there, so I pulled her into my lap. I needed to hug something.

"The terrible, scary part," I said to Hannie, "is a witch meeting. I don't know where Morbidda Destiny went last night. That doesn't matter now. But you heard her. When she was in the garden, she said, 'Midnight, important meeting, company's coming, we must be ready.' Morbidda Destiny is going to have a meeting of witches at her house at midnight tonight."

"No, no," said Hannie. "You're wrong, Karen. Morbidda Destiny was talking *to* Midnight the cat, not *about* midnight the time."

"Was not," I replied. "She meant midnight tonight. I'm sure of it."

"Oh, Karen!" exclaimed Hannie. "That *is* terrible."

44

"I know. That's what I said."

Shannon pushed her wet nose against my chin. She gave me a doggie kiss.

"Thanks, Shannon," I said. I felt better — but not much.

Shannon began to whine, so I put her on the floor.

Daddy and Elizabeth came into the kitchen.

"Hi, girls," said Daddy. "What have you been up to?"

I looked at Hannie. I opened my eyes wide. Spying.

"We were sp — ," Hannie started to say.

"Nothing," I said loudly. "What have you been up to?"

"Gardening," said Daddy. "I think I'll put a new flower bed in the front yard." (Daddy just loves to garden. It's his hobby. It's my grandma's hobby, too.) "Maybe I'll put an herb garden in somewhere, too. I should talk to Mrs. Porter about that."

"NO!" I shrieked.

I didn't *mean* to shriek so loudly. But I did. Daddy and Hannie jumped. Shannon skittered out of the kitchen. And Elizabeth dropped a glass. It broke.

"Oops," I said.

Sometimes I can be a pain in the neck.

"I'm sorry," I said to Elizabeth.

"Karen, for heaven's sake," she said crossly. "Was it necessary to scream like that?"

"Sorry," I said again.

"Don't come near the broken glass. You

stay away, too, Hannie. Let me clean it up. . . . Karen, why did you scream? Don't you want your father to talk to Mrs. Porter? She's perfectly nice. Your grandma is a good friend of hers."

I didn't want to think about Grandma being friends with a witch.

"Oh, I don't, um, like herbs," I lied. "Please don't grow them, Daddy. They're gross."

Daddy laughed.

"Come on, Hannie," I said. "Let's go to my room."

Hannie and I stood up.

"Watch the glass," said Elizabeth.

Hannie and I tiptoed out of the kitchen. Then we ran to my room.

"That was close," I said. "I didn't want Daddy to know we've been spying. But, oh, Hannie, just think. Tonight at midnight a whole flock of witches is going to be right next door to me!"

Witches and Warlocks

"Unh, two, fee, pit!"

It was bedtime again. Andrew and David Michael and I were leaning over the bathroom sink. We were looking at our toothpaste foam.

"Pretty good," I said.

"But not a record," David Michael decided.

"No," Andrew agreed thoughtfully. "Not a record."

We heard footsteps on the stairs.

"Rinse!" I ordered.

We rinsed out the sink.

"Bedtime!" Daddy called.

"Daddy? Can Kristy come up and read me a story?" I wanted to know.

"I'll ask her," said Daddy. He disappeared downstairs.

"Good night," David Michael and Andrew and I said to each other.

"Don't let the bedbugs bite," added Andrew.

"See you in the morning bright," I told him.

I went to my room and climbed into bed. Daddy and Elizabeth came in to say good night. They said good night to Moosie, too.

Then Kristy came in.

"Oh, goody!" I said. "Can you read *The Littlest Witch*, please?"

"What, again?" replied Kristy. "Why do you want to hear it? It always scares you."

I screwed up my face and thought. "Okay then. *Little Toot*," I finally suggested. But when we'd finished that, I still wanted to hear *The Littlest Witch*. So Kristy read it.

And she didn't skip any words. I could tell.
I'm a good reader.

"Kristy?" I said when she'd put the books
away.

"What?" Kristy sat on the edge of my bed
and played with Moosie's paws.

"I have to tell you a secret," I whispered
to her.

Kristy leaned closer.

"Tonight," I went on, "a witch meeting
is going to be held next door. At Morbidda

Destiny's house. A hundred, maybe even a thousand witches will be there."

Quick as a flash, Kristy pulled my window shade down. "Now don't go spying again tonight, Karen," she exclaimed. "You make yourself crazy. You imagine all sorts of things."

"I'm not imagining. I mean, I won't be. There really is going to be a witch meeting tonight."

"Warlocks, too?" asked Kristy.

"What are warlocks?"

"Boy witches."

"You mean there are boy witches?" I cried. "I didn't know that! This meeting could be huge!"

"Do you want to sleep in my room again?" Kristy asked me. "You look scared."

"I — I'm not scared," I said. (My teeth were chattering. *Boy* witches?)

"You sure *look* scared."

"Well, I'm not!"

Besides, I had a plan. And I couldn't do my plan in Kristy's room.

Kristy gave me a funny look.

"Thank you for asking, though," I said politely. "I'll be fine." I lay down and pulled my covers up.

"All right. Good night, then," said Kristy. "And good night, Moosie."

I held Moosie up. I danced him from side to side. "Good night, Kristin Amanda Thomas," I made him say.

The Witch's Spell

As soon as Kristy was gone, I snapped up my window shade. I looked at Morbidda Destiny's house. One light was on. That was all I could see.

I reached under my bed and pulled out an alarm clock. It was old. I'd found it in the basement. How did you set an alarm clock? I wasn't sure. But I wanted this one to wake me up at a quarter to midnight.

I fiddled around with the buttons on the back. Then I wound it up. When I was finished, I put the clock on the windowsill, right next to my bed. *Tick-tock. Tick-tock.*

This was my plan: The alarm clock would wake me up. I would look out my window. I would watch all the witches flying to Morbidda Destiny's house. I would watch them park their brooms on her roof and her lawn. I would watch them go inside. Then, if they started to do anything they shouldn't, I would wake up the whole neighborhood.

I would scream and yell. "It's the witches!" I would say. "The witches are up to their tricks. Quick! Run for your lives! Save yourselves!"

It was a great plan.

I would be a hero in Stoneybrook.

Probably, the mayor would give me a parade. I would get to ride in a car and wave to the people and wear a crown.

I closed my eyes and fell asleep.

I didn't wake up until 8:30 the next morning. That stupid alarm clock was looking right at me. It was ticking away cheerfully. But the alarm hadn't gone off.

I gasped. Morbidda Destiny must have put a spell on it! She must have figured out my plan. She didn't want me to wake up and warn everybody. So she said a witch's spell and burned a candle.

I bet she put a spell on everyone in the neighborhood, too! She must have done something so we would *all* stay asleep. That was the only way to hold a witch meeting, of course.

That darn old Morbidda Destiny, I thought. She was just too smart.

I wondered what had happened at the meeting. What had the witches talked about? What had they decided? Were they going to do anything to our neighborhood?

There was only one way to find out.

Spy.

Spy without getting caught, of course.

And today was my last chance to spy for two whole weeks. This afternoon, Mommy would pick Andrew and me up. We would go back to the little house.

I leaped out of bed. I took off my pajamas and put on my clothes.

I was going to have a busy day.

Caught!

I began spying right after breakfast. I had to be extra careful. Daddy was working in the garden again. Mostly, he was working in the front yard. But at breakfast he had said to my stepmother, "Perhaps the herb garden should go in the back, Elizabeth. If I started it near Mrs. Porter's garden, she could give me a hand from time to time."

Was Daddy crazy? Our own herb garden next to Mrs. Porter's? That meant two things. It meant Morbidda Destiny would come in our yard to look at our garden. And it meant her magical herbs might get mixed up with our regular ones.

On the other hand, having our own herb garden would mean *I* could get herbs whenever I needed them. Maybe I could learn to work some spells.

Anyway, I began my spying in the backyard. I really wanted to look at the front of Morbidda Destiny's house. But Daddy was in the front.

I stood behind a shrub and peered at the witch's back door. It was closed. I couldn't hear a sound.

I moved all the way back to the toolshed. When I looked around the corner of the shed I could see Morbidda Destiny's whole backyard and all of the back of her house. I searched the ground and the roof. I thought maybe I would see a forgotten broom. Or a lost hat. Or a black cat that didn't belong there.

Nothing.

How boring.

Crash! Bang!

I gasped. Someone — *or something* — was in our toolshed.

"Karen?" (It was Daddy. He must have heard me.)

I flattened myself against the side of the shed. I kept as still as a mouse.

"Karen?" Daddy called again.

I held my breath.

Soon I heard footsteps. Good. He was going away.

"Karen!" No, he wasn't. He'd found me.

"Hi," I said.

"What are you doing here?" asked Daddy. He sounded as if he thought I was doing something I shouldn't be doing. Like spying.

"Oh, I, um, I — I'm back here looking for my ring," I lied. "That beautiful ring I got from the Cracker Jacks box."

I knew Daddy would remember that ring. Andrew and I had had a big fight over it. We both wanted it. (Then Andrew got a tattoo prize in another box, so he kept that, and I kept the ring.)

I sat down on the ground and pretended

to look around. Daddy looked, too.

"Darn," I said.

"Why do you think the ring might be back here?" Daddy wanted to know.

I shrugged. "I've looked everywhere else."

Daddy stood up. "That's too bad, honey," he said.

"Oh, well, Maybe I'll get another one sometime. Thanks for helping me look!" I got to my feet and ran off.

Whew. Another close call.

The Witch Meeting

I waited until Daddy was in the front yard. Then I hid behind the shrub again. I watched and watched. Morbidda Destiny's house was as quiet as a tombstone.

Tombstone. Now there was a scary word. I wondered why I had thought about tombstones. Let's see. Graveyards . . . misty nights . . . ghosts . . . I felt a hand on my shoulder.

"Aughhh!" I screamed.

"Karen Brewer," said Kristy. "You're spying, aren't you?"

I whirled around. "Yes," I replied. "And you nearly scared me to death."

"It serves you right. You're not supposed to spy on the neighbors. You know that. It's a rule."

"Are you going to tell?" I asked.

"Maybe. Would you please stop it. I'm — "

Honk, honk!

"Oh, there's Mary Anne and her dad," said Kristy. "They're taking me downtown. Gotta go. See you later! And quit spying!"

Kristy ran off. I followed her partway. I watched her climb into the car with her friend Mary Anne Spier. Mr. Spier drove off. I waved.

As soon as the car was out of sight I headed for the shrub again. But then I saw Daddy. He was carrying his gardening tools into the backyard. Perfect. Now I could spy from the front.

The front is better for spying because there's a low hedge between our yard and

Morbidda Destiny's. And there's one spot where I can just fit between two of the bushes. Nobody can see me there.

I wriggled in.

Right away, things started to happen. The front door of the witch's house opened. Morbidda Destiny came out with a broom! Yikes!

She was dressed differently than usual. She was still in black, but she wasn't wearing

a shawl or robes. Just a long, old-fashioned dress. And her hair wasn't so frazzly.

She looked almost, well, nice.

But what was she doing with her broom? Oh. She was sweeping the front steps.

Did they *really* need sweeping? Or was she trying to make people forget she was a witch? I couldn't tell.

Morbidda Destiny finished her sweeping. She carried her broom inside.

A few minutes later she came out again. This time she was carrying a large pair of scissors. She marched herself over to a flower garden.

Snip, snip. Snip, snip. She cut the flowers until she had a gorgeous bouquet. Then she took the flowers inside.

What would happen next? I waited for a long time, but the witch did not come out of her front door again. Finally I heard voices. I peeked around the hedge, leaning way over. I could see all the way along the edge of Morbidda Destiny's yard. And there in the back was my witch. She was in her herb garden again. She was snipping away and talking to Daddy. After awhile, she went back inside.

Hmm, I thought. Morbidda Destiny had swept off her porch. She had cut flowers and more herbs. She seemed to be getting ready for something — but what? The witch meeting had been held the night before. Hadn't it?

Just then, three cars pulled up in front of Morbidda Destiny's house. I ducked back into the hedge. I held my breath. Who was going to get out of those cars? Witches?

Out of each car stepped an old woman. The women didn't look very witchy, but with witches, it's hard to tell. One was carrying a casserole dish. One was carrying a plate of cookies. The third was carrying some books and papers.

They rang Morbidda Destiny's bell and she let them inside.

A few more cars arrived. Some more

women and a couple of men got out. They were all carrying food and books and stuff.

Suddenly a thought came to me. It was an amazing thought.

I needed Hannie.

As fast as I could, I ran to her house.

At Hannie's House

Hannie Papadakis answered the door herself.

"Hannie! Hannie!" I cried. "You won't believe this!"

"What is it?" she asked.

"I was wrong about the witch meeting. Morbidda Destiny didn't hold it last night. She's holding it *right now*. When she said twelve o'clock, she meant noon today, not midnight last night."

"But I *heard* her say 'midnight,' " said Hannie, frowning.

"Oh, she was just talking to her cat."

"But you said — "

"Never mind that. Listen, the witches are all arriving right now. Some warlocks, too. I've been watching them."

Hannie's eyes grew wide. "You have? Where are they parking their brooms? I've always wondered about that." Hannie looked out the door.

"Well, that's the weird thing," I told her. "They're not coming on brooms. They're coming in cars. I don't know why. But they're having a meeting all right. They're bringing food and books and papers. The books must be spell books and the papers must have spells written on them. New spells that they need to practice."

"Are you sure?"

"Yes. And you know what?"

"What?" asked Hannie.

"We have to go over there. We have to stop the meeting. . . . We have to *save our neighborhood.*"

"Can't someone else do that?" asked Hannie.

"No one else knows about the witch meeting," I told her. "Besides, don't you want to be a hero? The mayor would give us a parade. Maybe even medals. We'd get to ride in a car and wave and wear crowns. The mayor would give everyone a day off from school, too."

Hannie looked like she couldn't make up

her mind. "That would be fun," she said slowly. "But I don't want to go in Morbidda Destiny's house. Do you? That would be crazy. They'll be praticing spells. You said so. They'd probably put a spell on *us*."

"Then we'll protect ourselves," I replied. I thought quickly. "Before we go into the witch's house, we'll go to her garden. We'll cut some herbs. We'll take them with us."

"I don't know . . ."

"And we'll make up our very own spell. A spell against witches."

"Oh, Karen . . ."

"What?"

"This just doesn't sound like a good idea, that's all. It sounds dangerous."

"Hannie. Don't you always do everything I say?"

"Yes," replied Hannie.

"And isn't it always okay?"

"No. Remember the time you said the Delaneys have so many jack-in-the-pulpits in their yard they'd never miss just one? So we dug one up, and Mrs. Delaney caught us. We were really in trouble. She liked those jack-in-the-pulpits."

"Well — " I began.

"And the time you said, 'Let's spray Noodle with perfume. It'll take his dog smell away.' Remember that? We used Mommy's good perfume. That was bad enough. But Noodle smelled awful, even after two baths."

"Aw, Hannie, I was just — "

"Besides, what do you know about witch spells and herbs?" Hannie asked me.

"Plenty," I told her. "Don't I live right next door to a witch? Don't I?"

"Yes."

"Believe me. I know enough. Now are you going to help me? Are you going to save our neighborhood? And be a hero?"

"I guess."

"Great!" I grabbed Hannie by the arm. I didn't want her to change her mind. "Let's go!"

"Wait. Let me tell Mommy and Daddy — "

"Don't you tell them anything!" I exclaimed.

Karen's Spell

I pulled Hannie out the door, across the street, and into my backyard. I did not see Daddy. Perfect.

Hannie and I stood at the edge of Morbidda Destiny's herb garden.

"We just need to take a few leaves," I said.

"Which ones?" Hannie whispered. "Spells always say things like a speck of cinnamon, and a pinch of, oh, garlic. How do we know what we need? And how do we know which is which?"

I frowned. "Stop asking so many questions. Any old leaves will do."

"But what about the magic? Aren't these magic herbs?"

"Of course. That's why they'll protect us. Now go get some stuff."

"*Me?* You go."

In the end, we each snatched a handful of green leaves. Together. Then we ran behind the toolshed. "Put them on the ground," I said. "We have to be careful with them. We'll leave them there while we make up a spell."

Hannie sniffed at her leaves. "They smell funny," she said.

"Never mind. Put them down for awhile."

We left the leaves in a little pile.

"Now for the spell," I said. "How about:

'Eye of bat and tail of . . .
        something,
Protect us from the witches'
        powers.' "

Hannie made a face. "If we say that, don't

we have to *have* the eye of bat and the tail of something?"

"Oh, yeah," I replied. "I guess so."

"How about this?" said Hannie.

> "Witches, witches, go away.
> Come again some other day."

"No!" I howled. "We don't want all these witches to come *back*."

"Oh, yeah."

I thought and thought. "All right," I said at last. "I think I've got one:

> 'Here are the witches.
> We'll give them a whack,
> So they can't hurt us.
> And they'll never come back.' "

"We'll give them a *whack?*" repeated Hannie. She looked afraid.

"I just mean with our spell. We won't really hit them. Now come on. We have to learn the spell — fast. Both of us. Because if there's any trouble at Morbidda Destiny's, this is what we'll do. We'll put the herbs in

our pockets." I picked up the leaves we'd taken from the garden. I gave half to Hannie and put the rest in my pocket. "If there's trouble," I went on, "you touch the herbs with one hand. With your other hand, you hold onto me tight. Then we say our spell together. Okay?"

"How does the spell go again?" asked Hannie.

I said the spell three more times. Then Hannie said it three times.

"Now, are you ready? I asked.

"Yes. . . . Ready for what? What are we going to do?"

"We're going to walk over to Morbidda Destiny's house. We'll ring her bell. When she answers the door, we'll march right into the meeting."

"We will?"

"Yes. And we'll say, 'Okay, all you witches and warlocks. We know what you're up to. You better leave our neighborhood alone.' See, Hannie? As soon as they know that *we* know what they're doing, they'll have to stop. It's simple. Let's get going."

"Oh, Karen," cried Hannie as I led her into the witch's yard. "I don't like this. I don't like it at all."

·Inside the Witch's House

Hannie and I tiptoed up to Morbidda Destiny's front porch.

"Please don't," said Hannie in a very small voice. "Please don't ring the bell."

I have to tell you something. I was pretty scared myself. I put my finger on the doorbell — then I pulled it away.

Hannie was watching me. "Good," she said. "Let's go."

I turned around. I looked at the street in front of the witch's house. Lots more cars had pulled up while Hannie and I were behind the toolshed. They were parked up and down the street.

My knees began to shake.

My mouth felt dry.

It was hard to speak, but even so, I said, "Hannie, look at all those cars. Think of how many witches and warlocks are inside Morbidda Destiny's house. Think of what they might be planning. We have to go in."

"Think of how much trouble we'll be in," said Hannie.

"We will *not* be in trouble," I told her. "We're going to get a parade and a day off from school. Maybe crowns and medals." I was *pretty* sure about this — but I wasn't positive. I just needed Hannie to come with me.

Hannie sighed. She did not say a word.

I touched the doorbell again. This time I pressed it. Hard.

Ding-dong.

"Oh, no . . ." moaned Hannie. She started to back away.

I grabbed her arm and pulled her toward me. "You stay right here," I said.

Just then, the door opened. Morbidda Destiny was standing in front of us, but I could hardly see her. She was dressed in black and she was standing in a shadowy hallway.

"Hey, heh, heh," she cackled. "Well, what have we here?"

"Hi, Mor — Mrs. Porter," I whispered. "Can we come in?"

The witch opened the door wider. She leaned over further. "What's that?" she asked.

I held my head high. "We'd like to come in," I said in a loud, haughty voice. But my insides felt scarder than scared.

"Well — Well —" Morbidda Destiny stammered. "Well, of course." She looked very surprised.

She also sounded nervous. That's what happens when you're trying to hide something.

Something like a witch meeting.

Morbidda Destiny did let us in, though.

"Karen," said Hannie as we stepped into the dark hallway. "Don't you think we should go home? It's lunchtime. I bet our parents are wondering where we are."

"It's too late," I whispered. "This meeting will be over soon. We have to talk to the witches now."

Morbidda Destiny was frowning at us.

She seemed confused. "What may I do for you?" she asked.

At least, I *think* that's what she asked. It sounded a little like she said, "What may I do *to* you?"

I looked at Hannie. I felt very afraid. I put my hand in my pocket and touched the magic herbs. They would keep me safe.

I spoke up in my loud, haughty voice again. "We would like to go to the meeting, please," I said.

"Ah," said Morbidda Destiny. "Certainly."

The witch walked down the hallway. It was dark, like the inside of a witch's house should be. I followed her. Hannie followed me. I kept one hand on the herbs. I put my other hand behind my back so Hannie could hold onto it.

I began to hear voices. The farther we walked, the louder the voices grew. I could hear talking and laughing.

I had to admit that the witches sounded awfully friendly.

Karen's Mistake

At last Morbidda Destiny reached the doorway to a big room. She stepped aside so Hannie and I could go in. I could see that I was right about one thing. A *lot* of witches had come to the meeting. There were so many of them that they couldn't all sit down. Every chair and couch was filled, and more witches were standing around. They were talking and laughing and eating. Some of them were looking through books about plants. Others were exchanging things that they'd written down on index cards.

Spells? Were they giving each other new *spells?* My legs felt like they were melting.

Hannie nudged me. "They seem nice," she said. "They look like they're having fun."

Hannie didn't look so scared anymore, but I felt awful. After all, I was the one who was going to have to do the talking. "Well, of . . . c-course," I replied nervously. "Witches are always nice to other witches. It's real people like us who have to worry. So keep your hand on your herbs."

"Okay," said Hannie.

"Now. I've got to make a speech," I said. "Ahem. Ahem. AHEM."

Some of the witches stopped talking and looked at me. But most of them didn't pay any attention.

"AHEM! AHEM!" I said again.

A few more stopped talking. Then more and more. The room was silent. Everyone was looking at me. Well, I *think* they were all looking at me. I couldn't see some of the ones in the back of the room.

Hannie was looking at me, too. Her look said, "Well, now what are you going to do?" I wasn't sure what I was going to do. I wanted to run out of that room and never think about witches again. But it was a little late for that.

"Excuse me," I said in a timid voice. "I want to — "

"Speak up!" called a man's voice. "Can't hear you."

"I want to say something," I tried to talk

more loudly. "My name is, um, is . . ."

"Karen!" Hannie whispered.

"Oh, yeah. It's Karen. And — and this is my friend Hannie. We know your secret. We know you're witches . . . and warlocks . . . " My voice was just trailing away. Everyone was staring at me. All those witch eyes and warlock eyes. I hadn't been so scared in my whole life.

The people just kept staring at us.

Finally one man said, "WHAT?" It sounded like an explosion.

Hannie began to cry. I felt like crying myself.

More voices were murmuring. But then a couple of the witches laughed.

"No, really," I said. I stood first on one foot, then on the other. "We — we know the truth. And H-Hannie and I have come to — to . . . Well, if you try to do anything to our neighborhood, we'll . . . we'll . . ."

I couldn't think of anything to say. And Hannie was just standing there crying.

"Well, we, um, we might tell our parents,

so . . ." I could feel my eyes filling with tears. More people were laughing. The others were just mad.

There was a commotion in the back of the room. I heard a gasp. I heard someone cry out.

"Oh, no!" I exclaimed. "Hannie, they're going to get us! Quick — the spell!"

Hannie had one hand in her pocket, touching the herbs. So did I. I grabbed for her other hand. "Now!" I said.

"Here are the witches," we whispered.

"We'll give them a smack," I heard Hannie say.

"Not smack, *whack*, Hannie! *Whack!* Start over!"

We started the rhyme again.

> "Here are the witches.
> We'll give them a whack,
> So they can't hurt us.
> And they'll never — "

"Karen Brewer!" cried a voice. It was a

familiar voice. Someone was pushing her way to the front of the room.

It was my grandma! Grandma Packett, Mommy's mother.

"It *is* you!" said Grandma. "I couldn't see from back there."

"Grandma!" I screamed. "*You're* a witch, too?"

I almost fainted.

Grandma knelt in front of me. She took me by the shoulders. "I am not a witch!" she said. She handed tissues to Hannie and me so we could dry our eyes. "Neither is anyone else here. This is a meeting of the Stoneybrook Gardeners Club. I don't know what is going on, but I want you to apologize, Karen. You, too, Hannie. Apologize to Mrs. Porter. Apologize to her guests. Then I'm going to take you home."

Uh-oh. I had a feeling Hannie and I were in trouble.

Big trouble.

Witch or No Witch?

I hate apologizing. At least it went quickly. As soon as Hannie and I had each said, "I'm sorry," Grandma hustled us outdoors. She seemed to be in a hurry.

"Now, Hannie, you go straight home, please," said Grandma.

"Okay," replied Hannie, sniffling. She ran toward her house.

"As for you, young lady, just what did you think you were doing?" Grandma asked me.

"Saving our neighborhood," I said in a very small voice.

Grandma set her mouth in a line. She was walking fast. I had to run to keep up with her. When we got to our front door, Grandma knocked. Then she opened it. She stuck her head inside. "Hellooo!" she called. "Watson? Elizabeth?"

Daddy and Elizabeth came running into the front hall. Of course, they were surprised to see Grandma. They were not expecting her.

"Mother Packett!" Daddy exclaimed.

He and Grandma hugged each other. Then Grandma told them about the gardening meeting. She told them what Hannie and I had done. Daddy and Elizabeth gasped. Their faces turned red. I didn't know if they were embarrassed or angry. Maybe both.

Oh, brother.

Grandma said that Hannie and I had already apologized to Mrs. Porter. She said she didn't know what we were up to, but that she had to go back to the meeting. She added that she hoped her friends wouldn't laugh at her too much. Then she left.

I looked around. Daddy and Elizabeth and I were not alone. Andrew, David Michael, and Kristy were peering at us from the living room. (When had Kristy come home?) Charlie and Sam were peering at us over the railing on the stairs.

"Karen Brewer," said Daddy in a low

voice. "I hope you can explain this."

Daddy looked very upset. I hadn't seen him look like that since the time I got in trouble for saying a bad word in a restaurant.

"I hope I can, too," I said. "See, um, Hannie and I thought, well, we thought that the meeting next door was — was a witch meeting. We kept seeing people with books and — "

"Were you spying?" asked Daddy. "Is that why you thought that?"

I glanced at Kristy. She didn't say anything. She was not going to tell on me. I would have to tell on myself.

"Yes," I said. "I was spying. So was Hannie. But it was my idea." I had dried my eyes with the tissue from Grandma, but now my eyes were filling up again.

David Michael took a step closer. "Is Karen going to get in trouble now?" he asked eagerly.

Sam and Charlie laughed.

"All right, kids," said Elizabeth to Kristy

and all my brothers. "Please go find something to do. Watson and I want to talk to Karen alone."

Daddy and Elizabeth and I went into the living room. We sat on the couch in a row. I was in the middle.

"You'd better tell us the story from the beginning," said Daddy.

So I did.

Daddy and Elizabeth just stared at me.

Finally Elizabeth said, "Oh, Karen."

That did it. My tears spilled over. They trickled down my cheeks.

"I'm sorry," I said. "I didn't mean to embarrass you."

Elizabeth and Daddy both sighed.

"We know that," Elizabeth said at last. "You thought you were helping the neighborhood. But Karen, honey, you have to understand that what you did was wrong. Imagine how Mrs. Porter feels now. You walked into her house and called her and her friends *witches*."

"That's another thing," said Daddy. "This witch business has gone too far. There are no such things as witches. Mrs. Porter is not a witch."

I nodded my head, but I didn't believe Daddy at all.

Daddy and Elizabeth looked at each other.

Finally Elizabeth said, "I better call Mrs. Papadakis. She should know what you and Hannie were up to. Mrs. Porter might call her later."

"I'm in big, big trouble, aren't I?" I asked.

"Not too big," Daddy replied. "Not this time. You thought you were doing something good, something brave."

"Right," said Elizabeth. "We can't punish you for that."

"But," Daddy went on, "you were spying, Karen. You did a lot of that this weekend. Don't we have a rule about spying?"

I nodded.

"What's the rule?" asked Daddy.

"No spying on the neighbors."

"Right," he said. "Or on anyone else. But you spied, and you got into a mess. So you owe Mrs. Porter an apology."

"I already apologized!" I exclaimed. "So did Hannie."

"You owe her a note," said Elizabeth.

Dear Witch

Daddy and Elizabeth helped me write a note to the witch. This is what it said:

Dear Mrs. Porter,
 I am sorry I ruined your meeting. I am sorry I called you and your friends witches. I did not mean it. I am VERY VERY sorry.

When the note was finished, Daddy said to me, "Promise me you won't spy anymore, Karen."

"Okay," I said.

"No," Daddy went on. "I want to hear you say it."

"I promise I won't spy anymore."

Daddy smiled. "Good girl."

I smiled, too. At least, I won't spy very much, I thought — only when I really have to.

It was time for Andrew and me to get ready to go back to Mommy's. We went to our rooms to pack our knapsacks. While I was saying good-bye to Moosie, Sam and Charlie came in my room.

"Heard any good spells lately?" asked Charlie.

"Better watch out or Mrs. Porter will make you grow a nose on your forehead," said Sam. He laughed loudly.

"Oh, you guys," I said with a sigh. "Hannie and I knew that was a gardening meeting. We knew it all along."

"Sure you did," said Charlie.

"We did! We just wanted to make Mrs. Porter smile. She's so lonely."

"Yeah, right," said Sam.

Sam and Charlie just laughed and laughed.

They laughed again when Mommy came and it was time for Andrew and me to say good-bye. Andrew and I hugged everybody. Kristy whispered to me, "I love you, Karen. Forget about witches."

Then we ran to Mommy and kissed her and climbed in the car.

As we drove away, I looked at Morbidda Destiny's house. I thought about the secret I knew. Mrs. Porter really was a witch. Maybe she *had* held a gardening meeting, not a witch meeting. But she was still a witch. After all, hadn't I seen her fly away on a broomstick?

Morbidda Destiny was a witch, a clever witch. And I was the only one who knew it.

About the Author

ANN M. MARTIN lives in New York City and loves animals, especially cats. She has two cats of her own, Mouse and Rosie.

Other books by Ann M. Martin that you might enjoy are *Stage Fright; Me and Katie (the Pest)*; and the books in *The Baby-sitters Club* series.

Ann likes ice cream and *I Love Lucy*. And she has her own little sister, whose name is Jane.

DON'T MISS OUT ON THE FUN!

Join Karen's Clubhouse Today!

Hi! It's Karen! If you love reading as much as my friends and I do, come join my clubhouse! It's easy! And members get lots of neat things, like:

- A "Karen's Clubhouse" doorknob hanger for your bedroom door! It has a list of all the Baby-sitters Little Sister® books on the back!
- An official membership card.
- Lots of cool stickers!
- Special tips on starting your own reading club with your friends!
- Plus, instructions for how to get a special "Karen's Reading Club" certificate!

Just fill in the coupon below and I'll enroll you into KAREN'S CLUBHOUSE. Please include $2.50 plus $1.00 to cover postage and handling.
Send to: Karen's Clubhouse, Scholastic Inc., P.O. Box 7500 2931 E. McCarty Street, Jefferson City, MO 65102. Return by December 31, 1994.

Karen's Clubhouse

☐ YES! Enroll me in Karen's Clubhouse! I've enclosed my check or money order (no cash please) for $3.50 made payable to Scholastic Inc.

Name _____

Age _____

Street _____   State _____ Zip _____

City _____

BSLS1193

88888888 LITTLE 🍎 APPLE 88888888

B·A·B·Y·S·I·T·T·E·R·S

Little Sister ™

by Ann M. Martin, author of *The Baby-sitters Club* ®

More Titles... ➡

The Baby-sitters Little Sister titles continued...

☐ MQ44825-0 #29	Karen's Cartwheel	$2.75
☐ MQ45645-8 #30	Karen's Kittens	$2.75
☐ MQ45646-6 #31	Karen's Bully	$2.95
☐ MQ45647-4 #32	Karen's Pumpkin Patch	$2.95
☐ MQ45648-2 #33	Karen's Secret	$2.95
☐ MQ45650-4 #34	Karen's Snow Day	$2.95
☐ MQ45652-0 #35	Karen's Doll Hospital	$2.95
☐ MQ45651-2 #36	Karen's New Friend	$2.95
☐ MQ45653-9 #37	Karen's Tuba	$2.95
☐ MQ45655-5 #38	Karen's Big Lie	$2.95
☐ MQ45654-7 #39	Karen's Wedding	$2.95
☐ MQ47040-X #40	Karen's Newspaper	$2.95
☐ MQ47041-8 #41	Karen's School	$2.95
☐ MQ47042-6 #42	Karen's Pizza Party	$2.95
☐ MQ46912-6 #43	Karen's Toothache	$2.95
☐ MQ47043-4 #44	Karen's Big Weekend	$2.95
☐ MQ47044-2 #45	Karen's Twin	$2.95
☐ MQ47045-0 #46	Karen's Baby-sitter	$2.95
☐ MQ43647-3	Karen's Wish Super Special #1	$2.95
☐ MQ44834-X	Karen's Plane Trip Super Special #2	$3.25
☐ MQ44827-7	Karen's Mystery Super Special #3	$2.95
☐ MQ45644-X	Karen's Three Musketeers Super Special #4	$2.95
☐ MQ45649-0	Karen's Baby Super Special #5	$3.25
☐ MQ46911-8	Karen's Campout Super Special #6	$3.25

Available wherever you buy books, or use this order form.

Scholastic Inc., P.O. Box 7502, 2931 E. McCarty Street, Jefferson City, MO 65102

Please send me the books I have checked above. I am enclosing $ _____
(please add $2.00 to cover shipping and handling). Send check or money order - no cash
or C.O.Ds please.

Name _____ Birthdate _____

Address _____

City _____ State/Zip _____

Please allow four to six weeks for delivery. Offer good in U.S.A. only. Sorry, mail orders are not
available to residents to Canada. Prices subject to change.   BLS793

THE BABY-SITTERS CLUB®

Claudia
Kristy
Mallory's
Stacey
Dawn
Mary Anne
Jessi

Wow! It's really them—
the new Baby-sitters Club® dolls!

Your favorite Baby-sitters Club characters have come to life in these
beautiful collector dolls. Each of your favorite character's style
comes through, down to her favorite jewelry and distinctive clothes.
A different book (that is not available elsewhere) is also included with each doll.

Look for the new Baby-sitters Club® collection...
coming soon to a store near you!

Kenner

The Baby-sitters Club © 1993 Scholastic, Inc. All Rights Reserved.   © Kenner 1993 a Division of Tonka Corporation Cincinnati, Ohio 45202

The purchase of this item will result in a donation to the Ann M. Martin Foundation, dedicated to benefitting
children, education and literacy programs, and the homeless.

Join the new online
Baby-sitters Club* on the
PRODIGY® service.

*A Custom Choice℠ for the PRODIGY service.

TALK TO ANN M. MARTIN IN A WEEKLY COLUMN

READ ALL NEW STORIES STARRING THE BSC GANG

VOTE ON STORY ENDINGS

MAKE FRIENDS ALL ACROSS THE COUNTRY

TAKE POLLS AND PLAY TRIVIA GAMES

For more information, have your parents call

1-800-776-0838 ext.261

PRODIGY is a registered service mark and trademark and Custom Choice is a service mark
of Prodigy Services Company. Copyright © 1992 Prodigy Services Company. All Rights Reserved.
Custom Choices are available at a monthly fee in addition to the monthly fee for the PRODIGY Service.

100 MILLION AND COUNTING...

Thanks to you loyal fans, there are more than 100 million Baby-sitters Club books in print!

NOW CELEBRATE WITH ONE OF ANN M. MARTIN'S BEST BABY-SITTERS CLUB STORIES EVER!

THE BABY-SITTERS REMEMBER
The Baby-sitters Club Super Special #11

by Ann M. Martin

FREE KEEPSAKE PIN!

It's a blast from the past, as the Baby-sitters, Shannon, and Logan share some of the memorable events of their lives with you! With a fab gold-foiled cover and a FREE BSC pin, this book is a must-have for every collection!

Foiled cover and free pin available while supplies last.

COMING TO A BOOKSTORE NEAR YOU!

THE BIGGEST BSC SWEEPSTAKES EVER!

Scholastic and Ann M. Martin want to thank all of the Baby-sitters Club fans for a cool 100 million books in print! Celebrate by sending in your entry now!

ENTER AND YOU CAN WIN:

• *10 Grand Prizes:* Win one of ten $2,500 prizes! Your cash prize is good towards any artistic, academic, or sports pursuit. Take a dance workshop, go to soccer camp, get a violin tutor, learn a foreign language! You decide and Scholastic will pay the expense up to $2,500 value. Sponsored by Scholastic Inc., the Ann M. Martin Foundation, Kid Vision, Milton Bradley® and Kenner® Products.

• *100 First Prizes:* Win one of 100 fabulous runner-up gifts selected for you by Scholastic including a limited supply of BSC videos, autographed limited editions of Ann Martin's upcoming holiday book, T-shirts, board games and other fabulous merchandise!

Just fill in the coupon below or write the information on a 3" x 5" piece of paper and mail to: **THE BSC REMEMBERS SWEEPSTAKES**, Scholastic Inc., P.O. Box 7500, 2931 East McCarty Street, Jefferson City, MO 65102. Entries must be postmarked by 10/31/94.

Send to Scholastic Inc., P.O. Box 7500, 2931 East McCarty Street, Jefferson City, MO 65102.

THE BSC REMEMBERS SWEEPSTAKES

Name _____ Birthdate _____

Address _____ Phone# _____

City _____ State _____ Zip _____

Where did you buy this book? ❏ Bookstore ❏ Other(Specify)

Name of Bookstore _____

BSCR194

ENTER SCHOLASTIC'S

THE BSC REMEMBERS SWEEPSTAKES

Official Rules:

No purchase necessary. To enter use the official entry form or a 3" x 5" piece of paper and hand print your full name, complete address, day telephone number and birthdate. Enter as often as you wish, one entry to an envelope. Mechanically reproduced entries are void. Mail to THE BSC REMEMBERS Sweepstakes at the address provided on the previous page, postmarked by 10/31/94. Scholastic Inc. is not responsible for late, lost or postage due mail. Sweepstakes open to residents of the U.S.A. 6-15 years old upon entering. Employees of Scholastic Inc., Kid Vision, Milton Bradley Inc., Kenner Inc., Ann M. Martin Foundation, their affiliates, subsidiaries, dealers, distributors, printers, mailers, and their immediate families are ineligible. Prize winners will be randomly drawn from all eligible entries under the supervision of Smiley Promotion Inc., an independent judging organization whose decisions are final. Prizes: Ten Grand Prizes each $2,500 awarded toward any artistic, academic or sports pursuit approved by Scholastic Inc. Winner may also choose $2,500 cash payment. An approved pursuit costing less than $2,500 must be verified by bona fide invoice and presented to Scholastic Inc. prior to 7/31/95 to receive the cash difference. One hundred First Prizes each a selection by Scholastic Inc. of BSC videos, Ann Martin books, t-shirts and games. Estimated value each $10.00. Sweepstakes void where prohibited, subject to all federal, state, provincial, local laws and regulations. Odds of winning depend on the number of entries received. Prize winners are notified by mail. Grand Prize winners and parent/legal guardian are mailed a Affidavit of Eligibility/ Liability/ Publicity/Release to be executed and returned within 14 days of its date or an alternate winner may be drawn. Only one prize allowed a person or household. Taxes on prize, expenses incurred outside of prize provision and any injury, loss or damages incurred by acceptance and use of prizes are the sole responsibility of the winners and their parent/legal guardian. Prizes cannot be exchanged, transferred or cashed. Scholastic Inc. reserves the right to substitute prizes of like value if any offered are unavailable and to use the names and likenesses of prize winners without further compensation for advertising and promotional use. Prizes that are unclaimed or undelivered to winner's address remain the property of Scholastic Inc. For a Winners List, please send a stamped, addressed envelope to THE BSC REMEMBERS Sweepstakes Winners, Smiley Promotion Inc., 271 Madison Avenue, #802, New York, N.Y. 10016 after 11/30/94. Residents of Washington state may omit return stamp.

HAVE YOU JOINED THE BSC FAN CLUB YET? See back of this book for details.

Don't miss out on
The All New

BABY·SITTERS®

Fan Club

Join now!
Your one-year membership package includes:

- The exclusive Fan Club T-Shirt!
- A Baby-sitters Club poster!
- A Baby-sitters Club note pad and pencil!
- An official membership card!
- The exclusive *Guide to Stoneybrook!*

Plus four additional newsletters per year

so you can be the first to know the hot news about the series — Super Specials, Mysteries, Videos, and more — the baby-sitters, Ann Martin, and lots of baby-sitting fun from the Baby-sitters Club Headquarters!

ALL THIS FOR JUST $6.95 plus $1.00 postage and handling! **You can't get all this great stuff anywhere else except THE BABY-SITTERS FAN CLUB!**

Just fill in the coupon below and mail with payment to: THE BABY-SITTERS FAN CLUB, Scholastic Inc., P.O. Box 7500, 2931 E. McCarty Street, Jefferson City, MO 65102.

THE BABY-SITTERS FAN CLUB

___ YES! Enroll me in The Baby-sitters Fan Club! I've enclosed my check or money order (no cash please) for $7.95

Name _____ Birthdate _____

Street _____

City _____ State/Zip _____

Where did you buy this book?

- ❑ Bookstore
- ❑ Book Fair
- ❑ Drugstore
- ❑ Book Club
- ❑ Supermarket
- ❑ other_____

BSFC593

THE BABY-SITTERS CLUB ®

by Ann M. Martin

More titles... ▶

❏ MG45659-8	#58 Stacey's Choice	$3.50
❏ MG45660-1	#59 Mallory Hates Boys (and Gym)	$3.50
❏ MG45662-8	#60 Mary Anne's Makeover	$3.50
❏ MG45663-6	#61 Jessi's and the Awful Secret	$3.50
❏ MG45664-4	#62 Kristy and the Worst Kid Ever	$3.50
❏ MG45665-2	#63 Claudia's Freind Friend	$3.50
❏ MG45666-0	#64 Dawn's Family Feud	$3.50
❏ MG45667-9	#65 Stacey's Big Crush	$3.50
❏ MG47004-3	#66 Maid Mary Anne	$3.50
❏ MG47005-1	#67 Dawn's Big Move	$3.50
❏ MG47006-X	#68 Jessi and the Bad Baby-Sitter	$3.50
❏ MG47007-8	#69 Get Well Soon, Mallory!	$3.50
❏ MG47008-6	#70 Stacey and the Cheerleaders	$3.50
❏ MG47009-4	#71 Claudia and the Perfect Boy	$3.50
❏ MG47010-8	#72 Dawn and the We Love Kids Club	$3.50
❏ MG45575-3	Logan's Story Special Edition Readers' Request	$3.25
❏ MG47118-X	Logan Bruno, Boy Baby-sitter Special Edition Readers' Request	$3.50
❏ MG44240-6	Baby-sitters on Board! Super Special #1	$3.95
❏ MG44239-2	Baby-sitters' Summer Vacation Super Special #2	$3.95
❏ MG43973-1	Baby-sitters' Winter Vacation Super Special #3	$3.95
❏ MG42493-9	Baby-sitters' Island Adventure Super Special #4	$3.95
❏ MG43575-2	California Girls! Super Special #5	$3.95
❏ MG43576-0	New York, New York! Super Special #6	$3.95
❏ MG44963-X	Snowbound Super Special #7	$3.95
❏ MG44962-X	Baby-sitters at Shadow Lake Super Special #8	$3.95
❏ MG45661-X	Starring the Baby-sitters Club Super Special #9	$3.95
❏ MG45674-1	Sea City, Here We Come! Super Special #10	$3.95

Available wherever you buy books...or use this order form.

Scholastic Inc., P.O. Box 7502, 2931 E. McCarty Street, Jefferson City, MO 65102

Please send me the books I have checked above. I am enclosing $_____
(please add $2.00 to cover shipping and handling). Send check or money order - no
cash or C.O.D.s please.

Name _____ Birthdate_____

Address _____

City_____ State/Zip _____
Please allow four to six weeks for delivery. Offer good in the U.S. only. Sorry, mail orders are not
available to residents of Canada. Prices subject to change.

Now THE BABY-SITTERS CLUB®

★ is a Video Club too! ★

JOIN TODAY—

- Save $5.00 on your first video!
- 10-day FREE examination-before-you-keep policy!
- New video adventure every other month!
- Never an obligation to buy anything!

Now you can play back the adventures of America's favorite girls whenever you like. Share them with your friends too.

Just pop a tape into a VCR and watch *Claudia and the Mystery of the Secret Passage* or view *Mary Anne and the Brunettes, The Baby-sitters and the Boy Sitters, Dawn Saves the Trees* or any of the girls' many exciting, fun-packed adventures.

Don't miss this chance to actually see and hear Kristy, Stacey, Mallory, Jessi and the others in this new video series. Full details below.

■■ ■■■ CUT OUT AND MAIL TODAY! ■■■ ■ ■

MAIL TO: Baby-sitters Video Club • P.O. Box 30628 • Tampa, FL 33630-0628

Please enroll me as a member of the Baby-sitters Video Club and send me the first video, *Mary Anne and the Brunettes* for only $9.95 plus $2.50 shipping and handling. I will then receive other video adventures—one approximately every other month—at the regular price of $14.95 plus $2.50 shipping/handling each for a 10-day FREE examination. There is never any obligation to buy anything.

NAME   PLEASE PRINT

ADDRESS   APT.

CITY

STATE   ZIP

BIRTH DATE

( )
AREA CODE   DAYTIME PHONE NUMBER

CHECK ONE:
☐ I enclose $9.95 plus $2.50 shipping/handling.
☐ Charge to my card: ☐ VISA ☐ MASTERCARD ☐ AMEX

Card number_____   Expiration Date_____

Parent's signature:_____   9AP S6

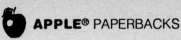

APPLE® PAPERBACKS

ANN M. MARTIN
author of your favorite series

Don't miss any of these great Apple® Paperbacks

❏ MW43622-8	**Bummer Summer**	**$2.95**
❏ MW45917-1	**Eleven Kids One Summer**	**$2.95**
❏ MW43621-X	**Inside Out**	**$2.95**
❏ MW43828-X	**Ma and Pa Dracula**	**$2.95**
❏ MW43618-X	**Me and Katie (the Pest)**	**$2.95**
❏ MW43136-6	**Missing Since Monday**	**$2.95**
❏ MW43619-8	**Stage Fright**	**$2.95**
❏ MW43620-1	**Ten Kids, No Pets**	**$3.25**
❏ MW43625-2	**With You and Without You**	**$2.95**
❏ MW42809-8	**Yours Turly, Shirley**	**$2.95**

Available wherever you buy books... or use this order form.

Scholastic Inc., P.O. Box 7502, 2931 East McCarty Street, Jefferson City, MO 65102

Please send me the books I have checked above. I am enclosing $———— (please add $2.00 to cover shipping and handling). Send check or money order — no cash or C.O.D.s please.

Name————————————————————————————————

Address —————————————————————————————————

City————————————————— State/Zip————————————————

Please allow four to six weeks for delivery. Offer good in the U.S. only. Sorry, mail orders are not available to residents of Canada. Prices subject to change.

AM1293

Create Your Own Mystery Stories!

THE BABY-SITTERS CLUB®

MYSTERY GAME !

WHO: Boyfriend   **WHY:** Romance
WHAT: Phone Call   **WHERE:** Dance

Use the special Mystery Case card to pick WHO did it, WHAT was involved, WHY it happened and WHERE it happened. Then dial secret words on your Mystery Wheels to add to the story! Travel around the special Stoneybrook map gameboard to uncover your friends' secret word clues! Finish four baby-sitting jobs and find out all the words to win. Then have everyone join in to tell the story!

YOU'LL FIND THIS
GREAT MILTON BRADLEY GAME
AT TOY STORES AND BOOKSTORES
NEAR YOU!

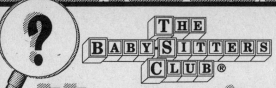

THE BABY-SITTERS CLUB®

Mysteries

by Ann M. Martin

Something mysterious is going on in Stoneybrook, and now you can solve the case with the Baby-sitters! Collect and read these exciting mysteries along with your favorite Baby-sitters Club books!

☐	BAI44084-5	#1	**Stacey and the Missing Ring**	$3.50
☐	BAI44085-3	#2	**Beware, Dawn!**	$3.50
☐	BAI44799-8	#3	**Mallory and the Ghost Cat**	$3.50
☐	BAI44800-5	#4	**Kristy and the Missing Child**	$3.50
☐	BAI44801-1	#5	**Mary Anne and the Secret in the Attic**	$3.50
☐	BAI44961-3	#6	**The Mystery at Claudia's House**	$3.50
☐	BAI44960-5	#7	**Dawn and the Disappearing Dogs**	$3.50
☐	BAI44959-1	#8	**Jessi and the Jewel Thieves**	$3.50
☐	BAI44958-3	#9	**Kristy and the Haunted Mansion**	$3.50
☐	BAI45696-2	#10	**Stacey and the Mystery Money**	$3.50
☐	BAI47049-3	#11	**Claudia and the Mystery at the Museum**	$3.50
☐	BAI47050-7	#12	**Dawn and the Surfer Ghost**	$3.50
☐	BAI47051-1	#13	**Mary Anne and the Library Mystery**	$3.50
☐	BAI47052-3	#14	**Stacey and the Mystery at the Mall**	$3.50

Available wherever you buy books, or use this order form.

Scholastic Inc., P.O. Box 7502, 2931 East McCarty Street, Jefferson City, MO 65102

Please send me the books I have checked above. I am enclosing $ _____ (please add $2.00 to cover shipping and handling). Send check or money order — no cash or C.O.D.s please.

Name _____ Birthdate _____

Address _____

City _____ State/Zip _____

Please allow four to six weeks for delivery. Offer good in the U.S. only. Sorry, mail orders are not availabl...
residents of Canada. Prices subject to change.

BSCM1193